TOBY THE TRAM ENGINE

by

The Rev. W. Awdry

with illustrations by
C. Reginald Dalby

Grolier

Toby and the Stout Gentleman

TOBY is a Tram Engine. He is short and sturdy. He has cow-catchers and side-plates, and doesn't look like a steam engine at all. He takes trucks from farms and factories to the main line, and the big engines take them to London and elsewhere. His tramline runs along roads and through fields and villages. Toby rings his bell cheerfully to everyone he meets.

He has a coach called Henrietta, who has seen better days. She complains because she has few passengers. Toby is attached to Henrietta and always takes her with him.

"She might be useful one day," he says.

"It's not fair at all!" grumbles Henrietta as the buses roar past full of passengers. She remembers that she used to be full, and nine trucks would rattle behind her.

Now there are only three or four, for the farms and factories send their goods mostly by lorry.

Toby is always careful on the road. The cars, buses and lorries often have accidents. Toby hasn't had an accident for years, but the buses are crowded, and Henrietta is empty.

"I can't understand it," says Toby the Tram Engine.

People come to see Toby, but they come by bus. They stare at him. "Isn't he quaint!" they say, and laugh. They make him so cross.

One day a car stopped close by, and a little boy jumped out. "Come on, Bridget," he called to his sister, and together they ran across to Toby. Two ladies and a stout gentleman followed. The gentleman looked important, but nice.

The children ran back. "Come on, Grandfather, do look at this engine," and seizing his hands they almost dragged him along.

"That's a tram engine, Stephen," said the stout gentleman.

"Is it electric?" asked Bridget.

"Whoosh!" hissed Toby crossly.

"Sh!" said her brother, "you've offended him."

"But trams *are* electric, aren't they?"

"They are mostly," the stout gentleman

answered, "but this is a steam tram."

"May we go in it, Grandfather? Please!"

The guard had begun to blow his whistle.

"Stop," said the stout gentleman, and raised his hand. The guard, surprised, opened his mouth, and the whistle fell out.

While he was picking it up, they all scrambled into Henrietta.

"Hip Hip Hurray!" chanted Henrietta, and she rattled happily behind.

Toby did not sing. "Electric indeed! Electric indeed," he snorted. He was very hurt.

The stout gentleman and his family got out at the Junction, but waited for Toby to take them back to their car.

"What is your name?" asked the stout gentleman.

"Toby, Sir."

"Thank you, Toby, for a very nice ride."

"Thank *you*, Sir," said Toby politely. He felt better now. "This gentleman," he thought, "is a gentleman who knows how to speak to engines."

The children came every day for a fortnight. Sometimes they rode with the guard, sometimes in empty trucks, and on the last day of all the driver invited them into his cab.

All were sorry when they had to go away.

Stephen and Bridget said "Thank you" to Toby, his driver, his fireman, and the guard.

The stout gentleman gave them all a present.

"Peep pip pip peep," whistled Toby. "Come again soon."

"We will, we will," called the children, and they waved till Toby was out of sight.

The months passed. Toby had few trucks, and fewer passengers.

"Our last day, Toby," said his driver sadly one morning. "The Manager says we must close tomorrow."

That day Henrietta had more passengers than she could manage. They rode in the trucks and crowded in the brake-van, and the guard hadn't enough tickets to go round.

The passengers joked and sang, but Toby and his driver wished they wouldn't.

"Goodbye, Toby," said the passengers afterwards, "we are sorry your line is closing down."

"So am I," said Toby sadly.

The last passenger left the station, and Toby puffed slowly to his shed.

"Nobody wants me," he thought, and went unhappily to sleep.

Next morning the shed was flung open, and he woke with a start to see his fireman dancing a jig outside. His driver, excited, waved a piece of paper.

"Wake up, Toby," they shouted, "and listen to this; it's a letter from the stout gentleman."

Toby listened and . . . *But I mustn't tell you any more, or I should spoil the next story.*

Thomas in Trouble

THERE is a line to a quarry at the end of Thomas's Branch; it goes for some distance along the road.

Thomas was always very careful here in case anyone was coming.

"Peep pip peep!" he whistled; then the people got out of the way, and he puffed slowly along, with his trucks rumbling behind him.

Early one morning there was no one on the road, but a large policeman was sitting on the grass close to the line. He was shaking a stone from his boot.

Thomas liked policemen. He had been a great friend of the Constable who used to live in the village; but he had just retired.

Thomas expected that the new Constable would be friendly too.

"Peep peep," he whistled, "good morning."

The policeman jumped and dropped his boot. He scrambled up, and hopped round on one leg till he was facing Thomas.

Thomas was sorry to see that he didn't look friendly at all. He was red in the face and very cross.

The policeman wobbled about, trying to keep his balance.

"Disgraceful!" he spluttered. "I didn't sleep a wink last night, it was so quiet, and now engines come whistling suddenly behind me! My first day in the country too!"

He picked up his boot and hopped over to Thomas.

"I'm sorry, Sir," said Thomas, "I only said 'good morning'."

The policeman grunted, and, leaning against Thomas's buffer, he put his boot on.

He drew himself up and pointed to Thomas.

"Where's your cow-catcher?" he asked accusingly.

"But I don't catch cows, Sir!"

"Don't be funny!" snapped the policeman. He looked at Thomas's wheels. "No side-plates either," and he wrote in his notebook.

"Engines going on Public Roads must have their wheels covered, and a cow-catcher in front. You haven't, so you are Dangerous to the Public."

"Rubbish!" said his driver, "we've been along here hundreds of times and never had an accident."

"That makes it worse," the policeman answered. He wrote "regular law breaker" in his book.

Thomas puffed sadly away.

The Fat Controller was having breakfast. He was eating toast and marmalade. He had the newspaper open in front of him, and his wife had just given him some more coffee.

The butler knocked and came in.

"Excuse me, Sir, you are wanted on the telephone."

"Bother that telephone!" said the Fat Controller.

"I'm sorry, my dear," he said a few minutes later, "Thomas is in trouble with the police, and I must go at once."

He gulped down his coffee and hurried from the room.

At the Junction, Thomas's driver told the Fat Controller what had happened.

"Dangerous to the Public indeed; we'll see about that!" and he climbed grimly into Annie the coach.

The policeman was on the platform at the other end. The Fat Controller spoke to him at once, and a crowd collected to listen.

Other policemen came to see what was happening and the Fat Controller argued with them too; but it was no good.

"The Law is the Law," they said, "and we can't change it."

The Fat Controller felt exhausted.

He mopped his face.

"I'm sorry, driver," he said, "it's no use arguing with policemen. We will have to make those cow-catcher things for Thomas, I suppose."

"Everyone will laugh, Sir," said Thomas sadly, "they'll say I look like a tram."

The Fat Controller stared, then he laughed.

"Well done, Thomas! Why didn't I think of it before? We want a Tram Engine! When I was on my holiday, I met a nice little engine called Toby. He hasn't enough work to do, and needs a change. I'll write to his Controller at once."

A few days later Toby arrived.

"That's a good engine," said the Fat Controller, "I see you've brought Henrietta."

"You don't mind, do you, Sir?" asked Toby anxiously. "The Station-Master wanted to use her as a hen house, and that would never do."

"No, indeed," said the Fat Controller gravely, "we couldn't allow that."

Toby made the trucks behave even better than Thomas did.

At first Thomas was jealous, but he was so pleased when Toby rang his bell and made the policeman jump that they have been firm friends ever since.